THAT'S NOT YOUR MOMMY ANYMORE

A Zombie Tale

MATT MOGK

Illustrated by
AJA WELLS

Ulysses Press

To my Great Aunt Marion—
I miss you a ton, but hope you never come back.

Published in the United States by
ULYSSES PRESS
P.O. Box 3440
Berkeley, CA 94703
www.ulyssespress.com

ISBN: 978-1-56975-926-4
Library of Congress Control Number 2011922512

Printed in the United States by Bang Printing

10 9 8 7 6 5 4 3 2

Acquisitions editor: Kelly Reed
Managing editor: Claire Chun
Proofreader: Lauren Harrison
Cover design: what!design @ whatweb.com
Production: Abby Reser

Distributed by Publishers Group West

Mommy has the kindest eyes.
Mommy likes to bake you pies.

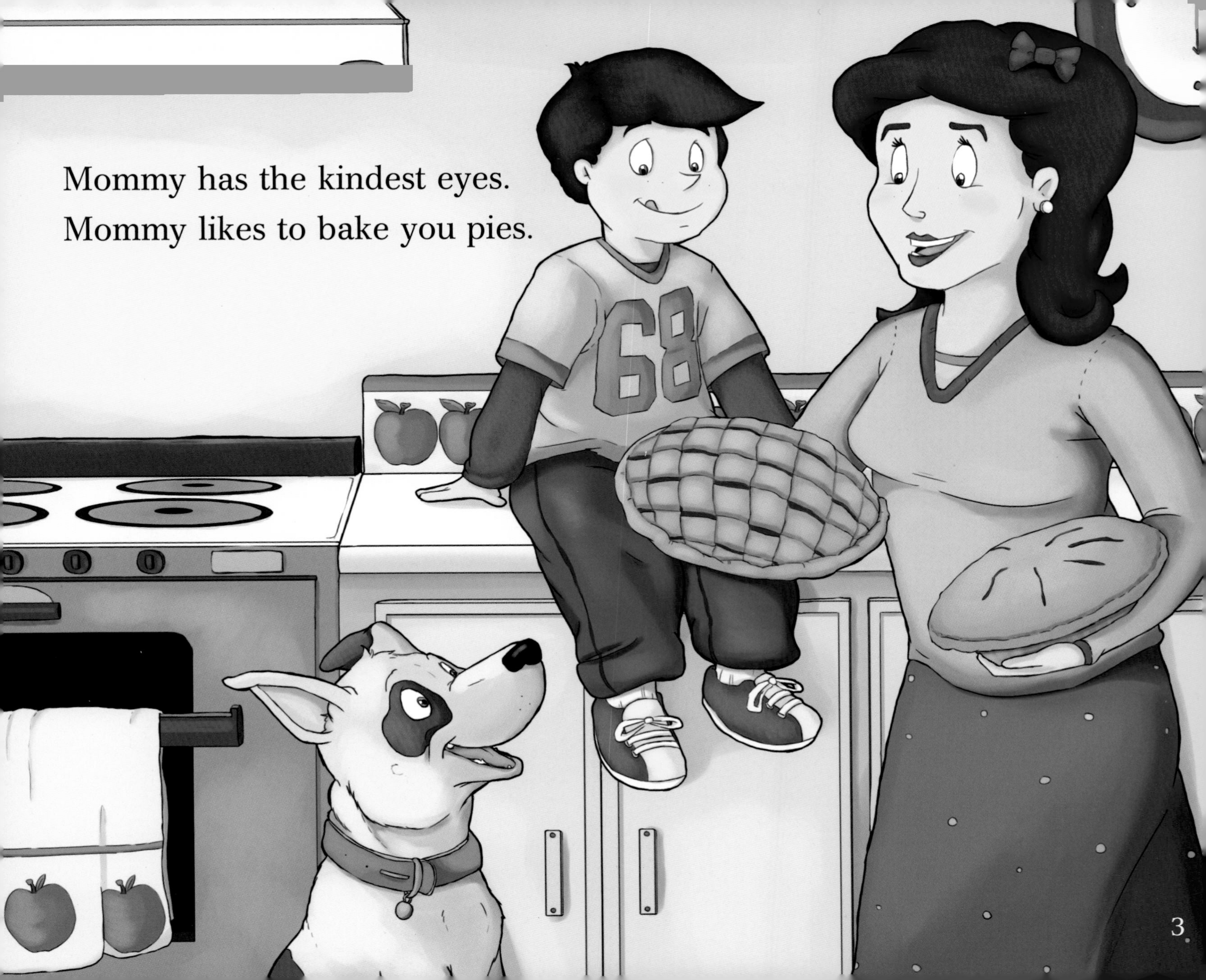

68

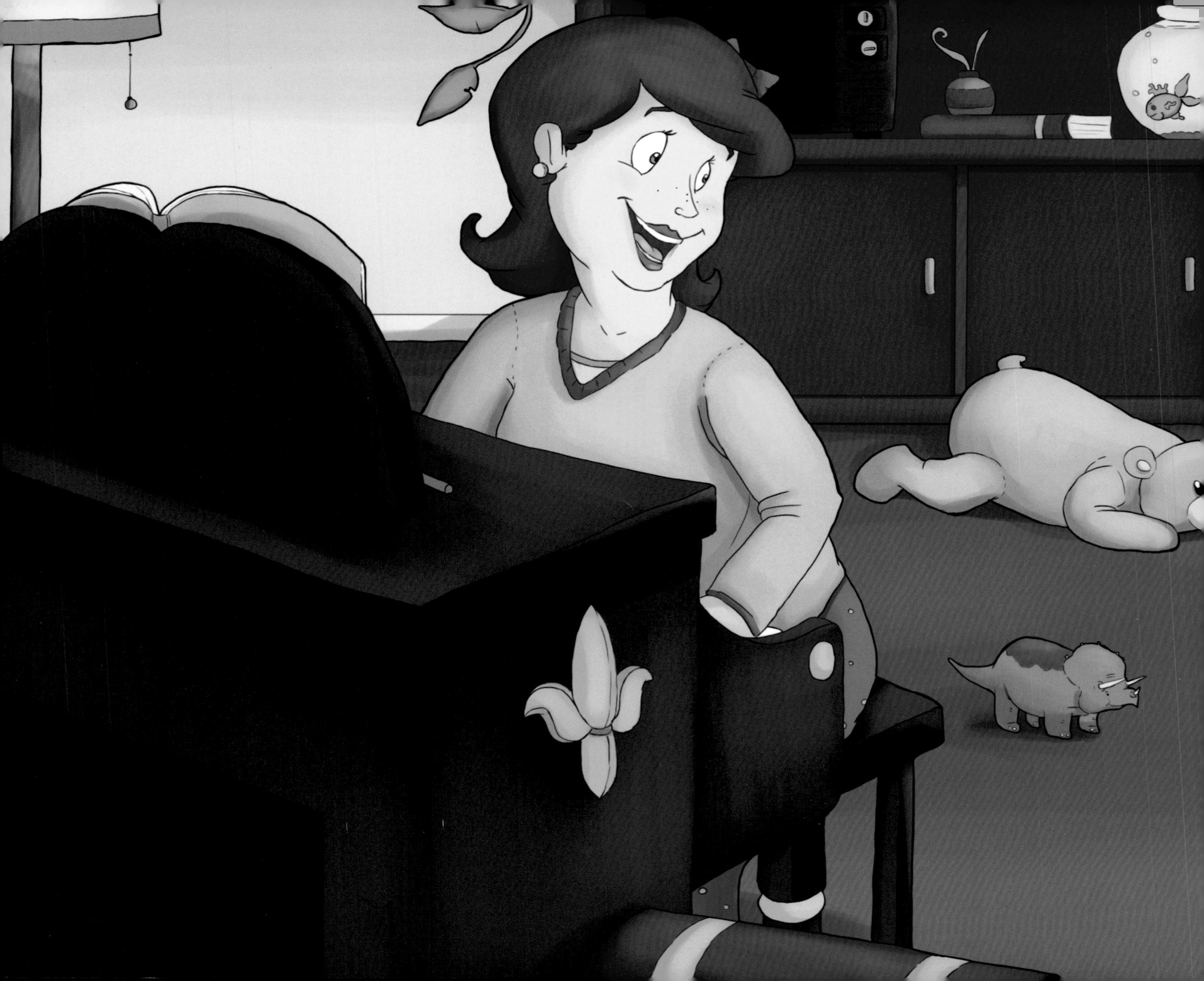

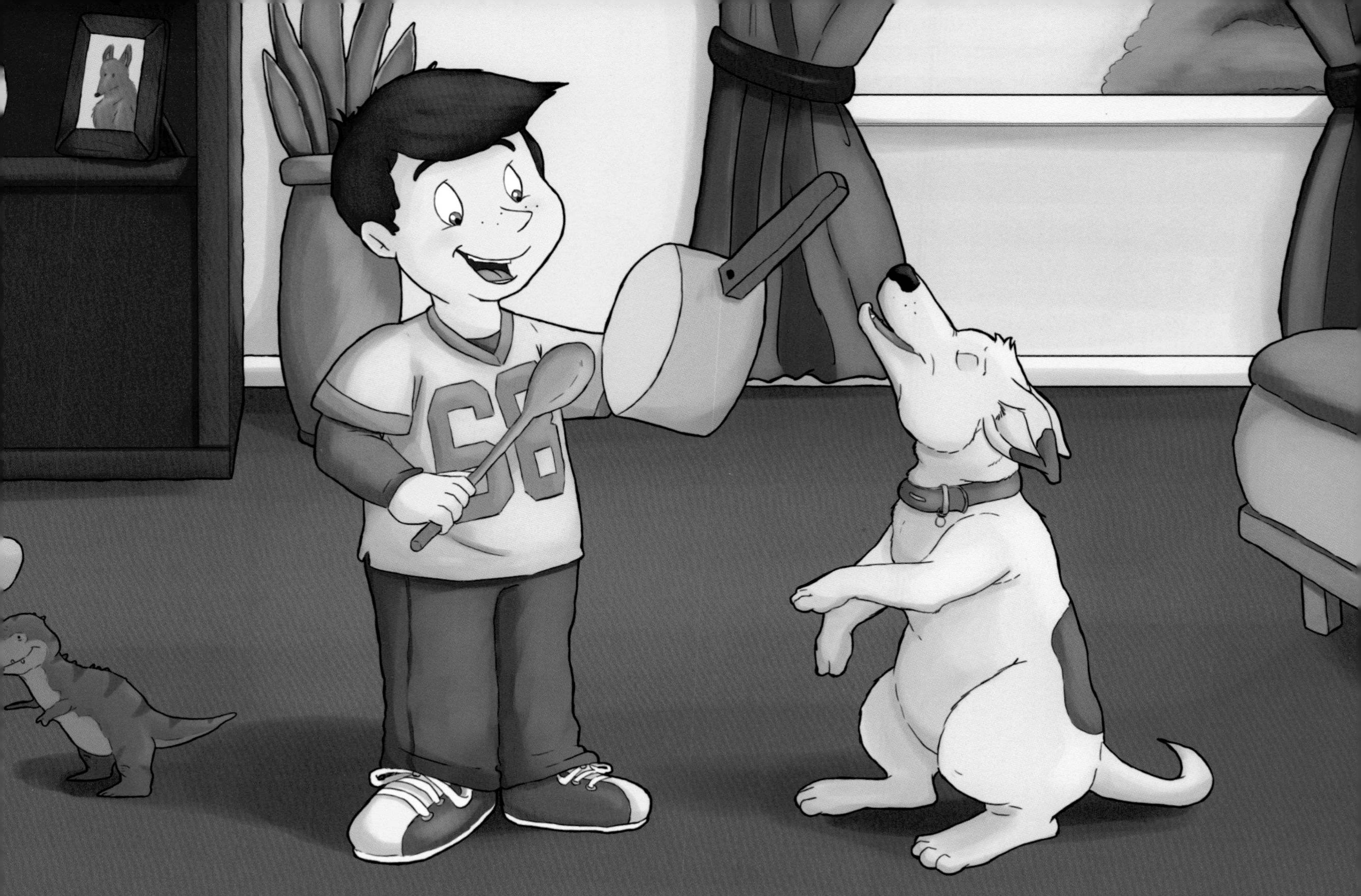

Mommy sings the sweetest songs.
Mommy lets you sing along.

Even when you're really bad
and do something to make her mad,

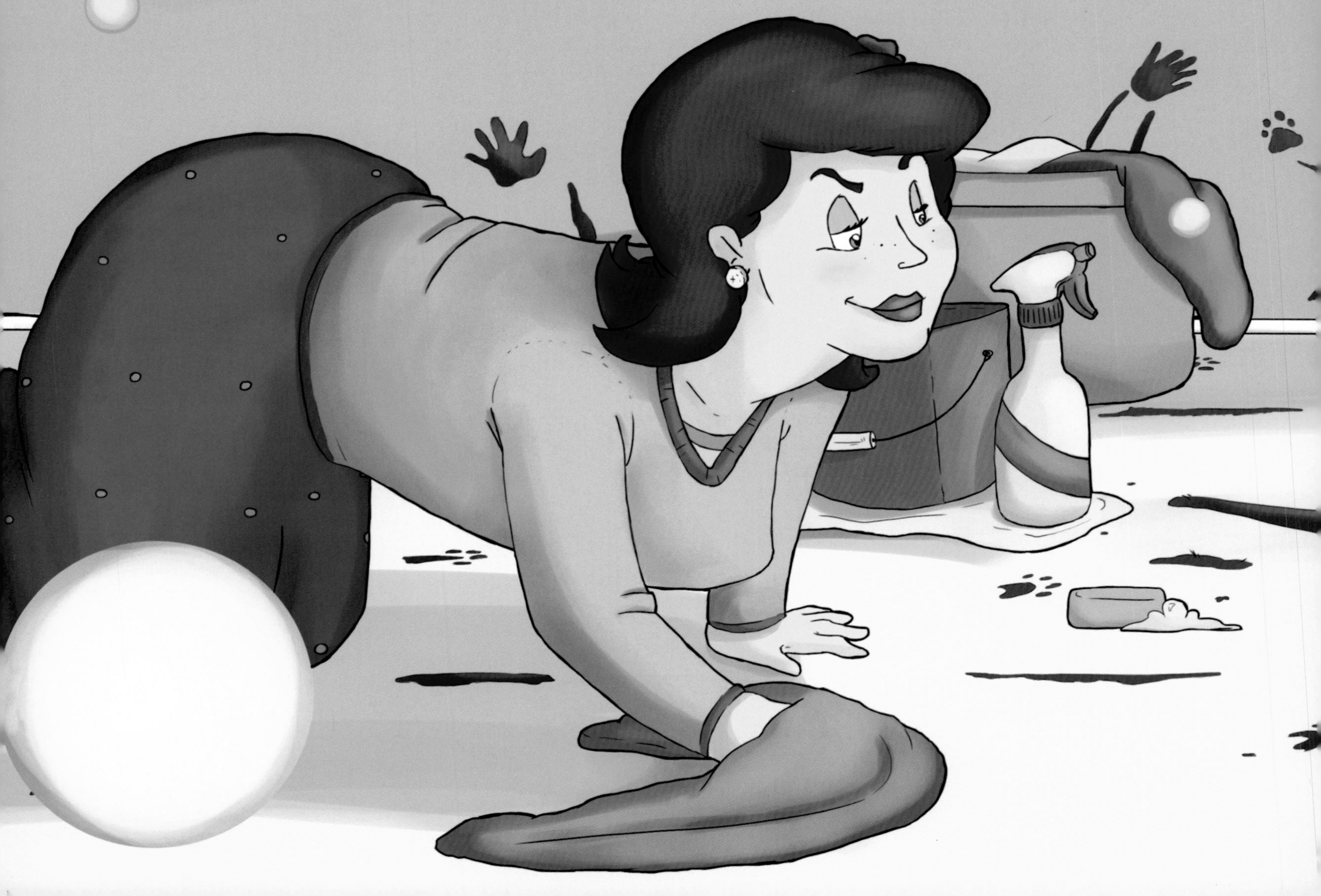

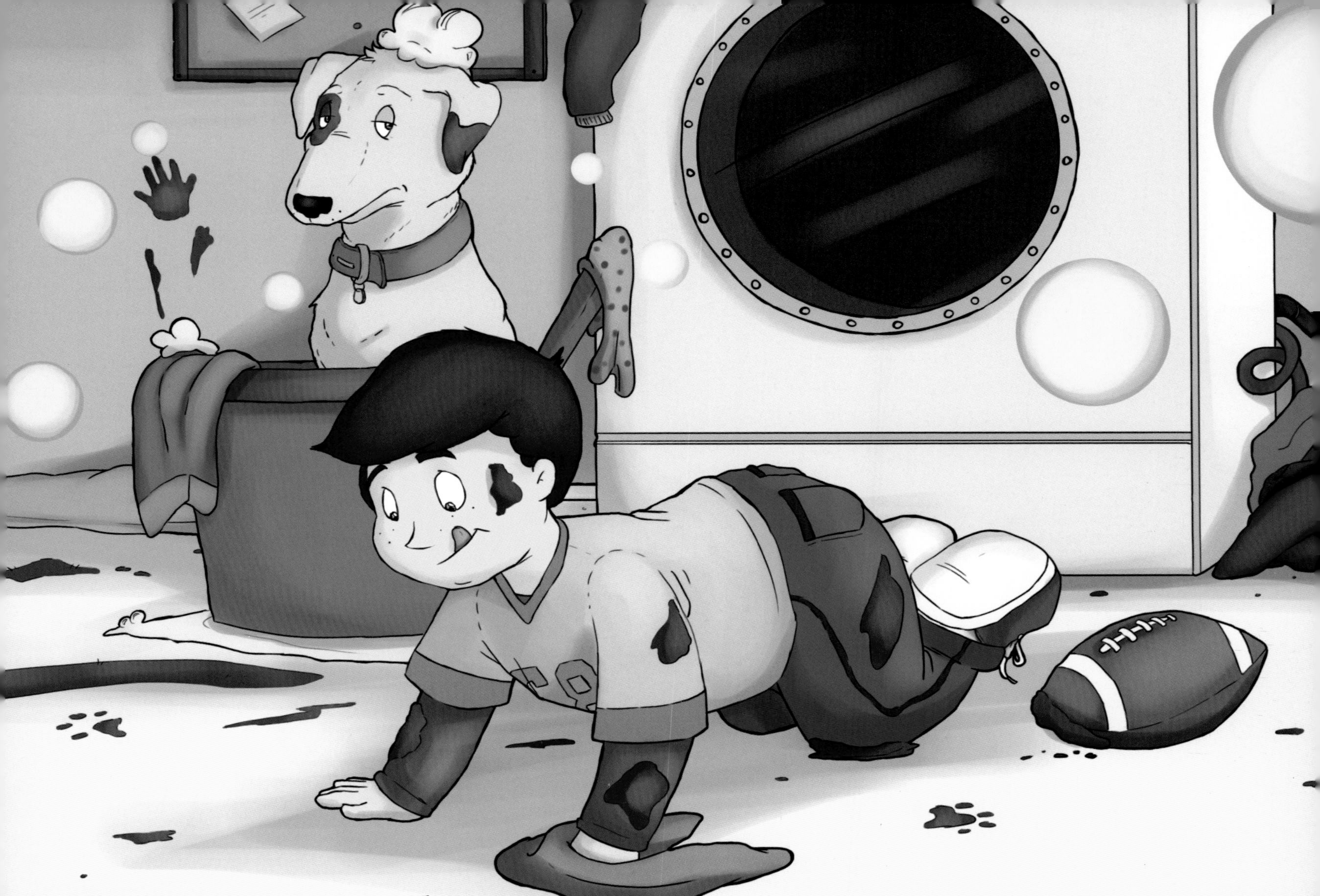

Mommy never stays that way
and soon enough she lets you play.

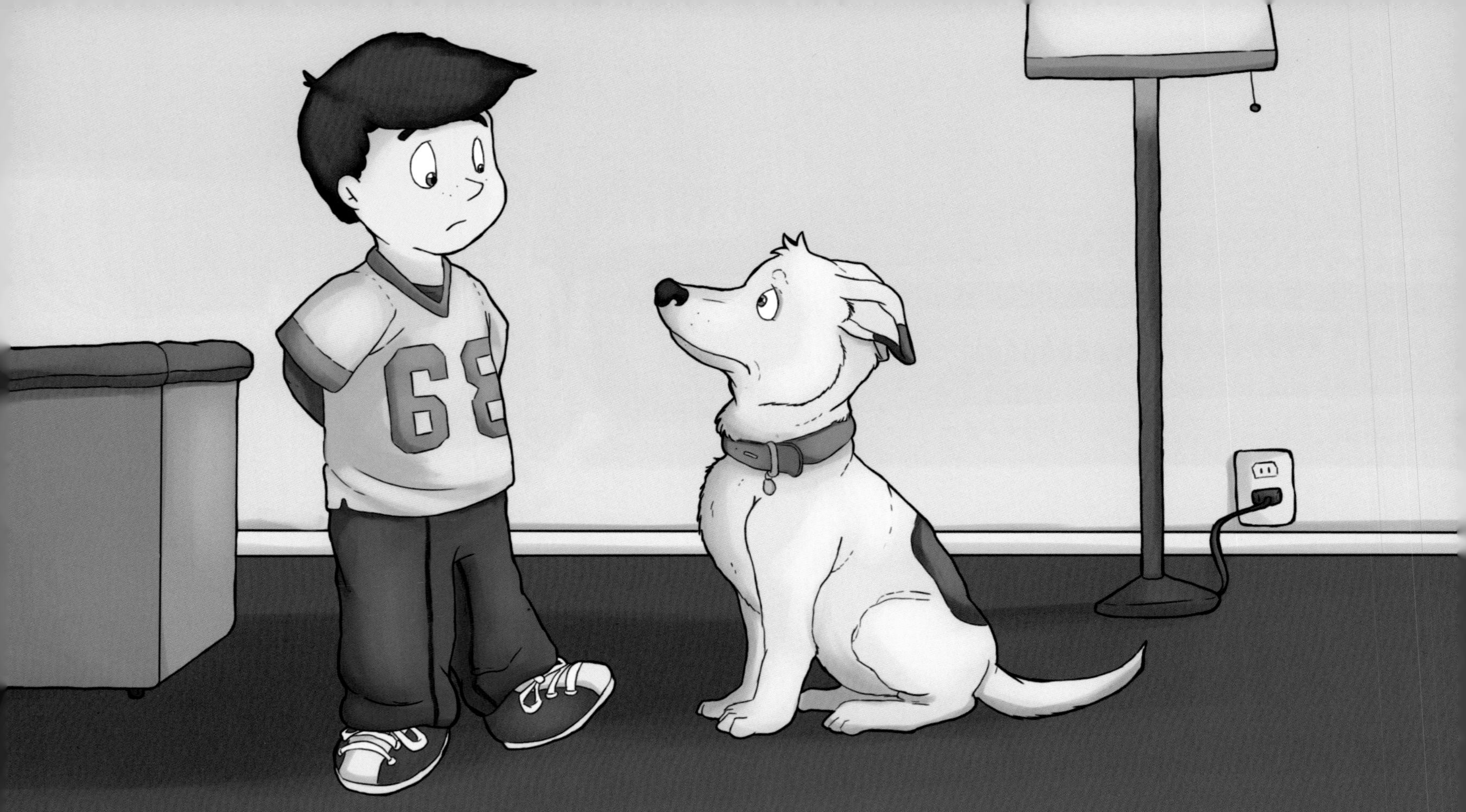

But if your Mommy's acting strange
and going through some kind of change,

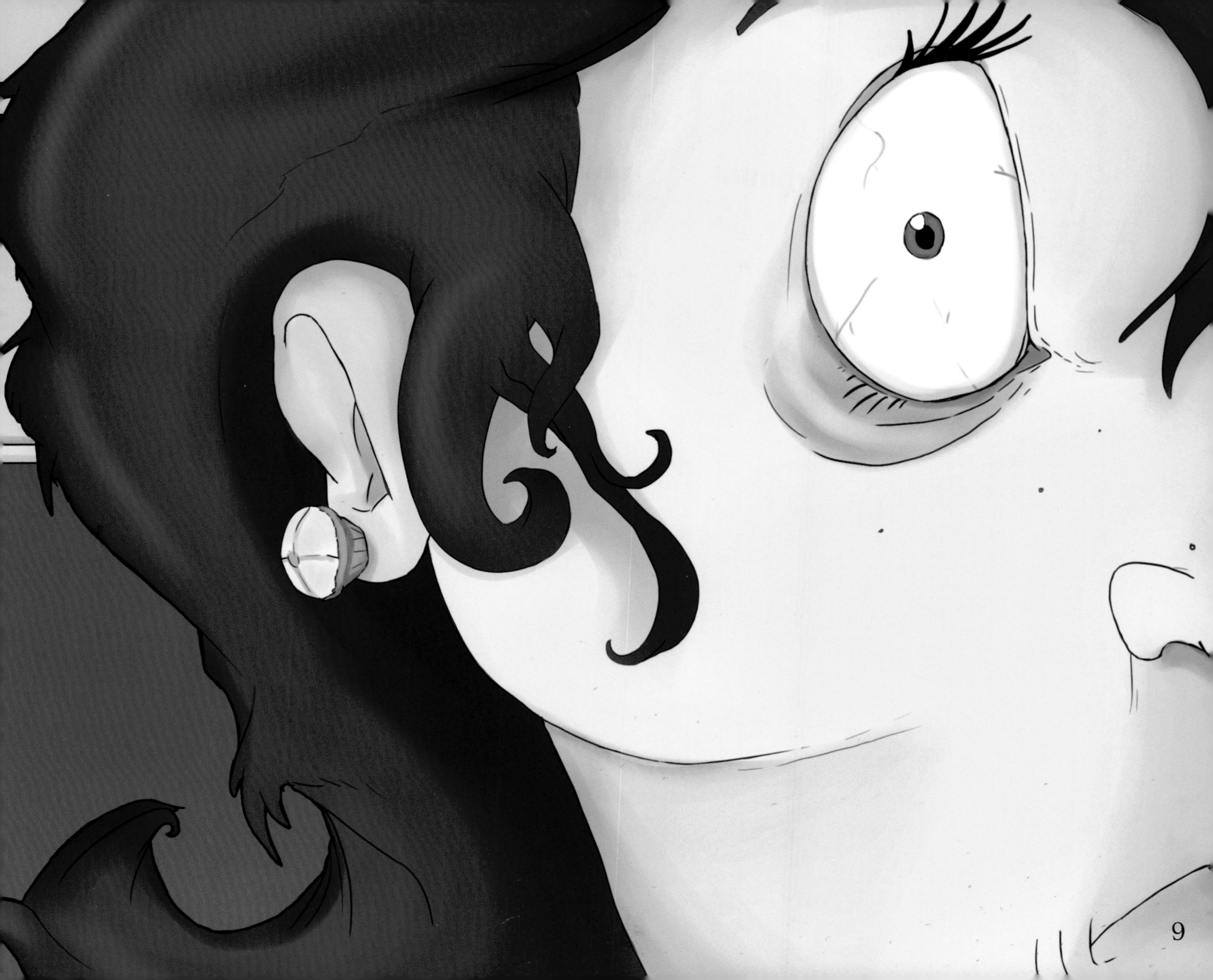

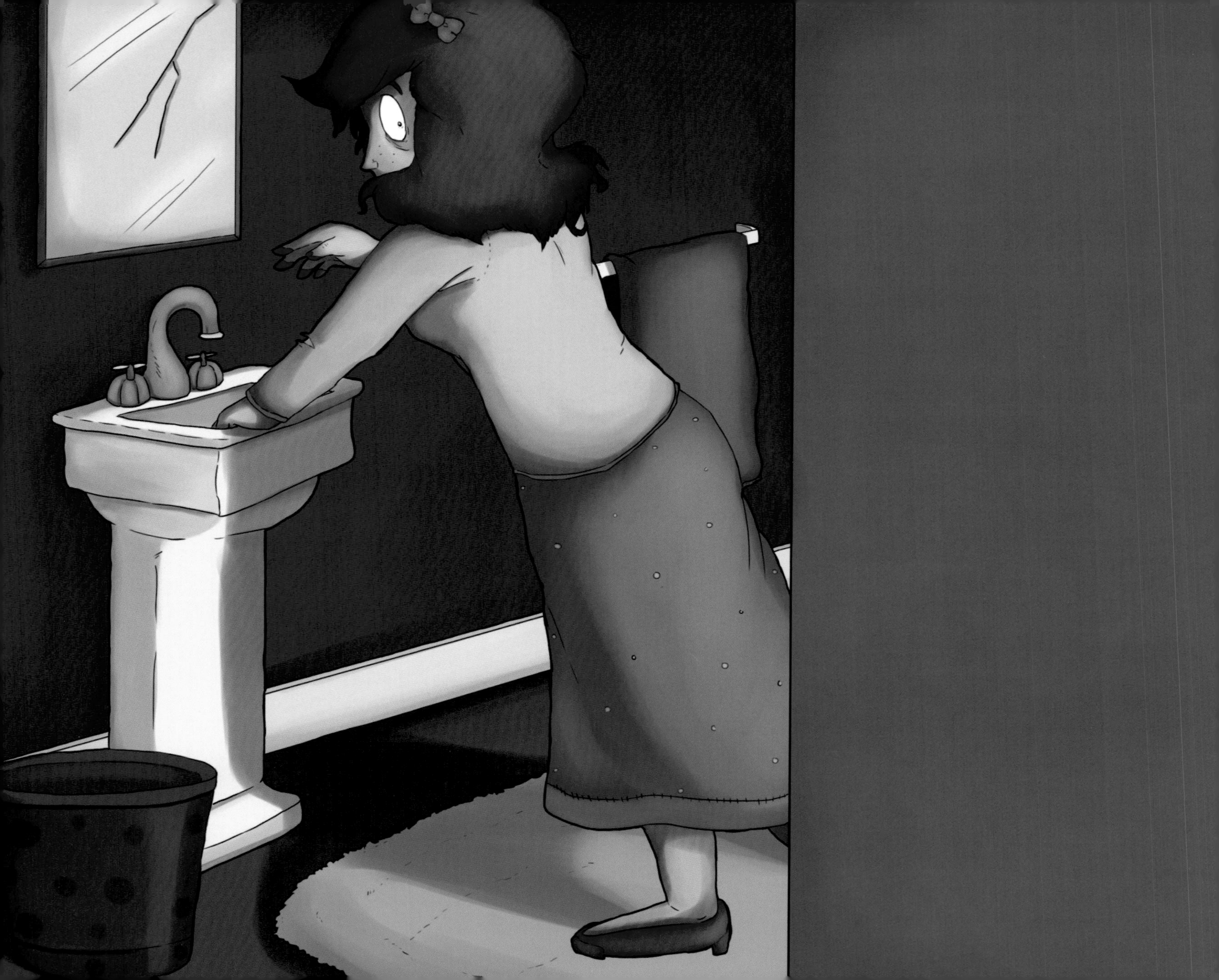

If she doesn't seem like she did before,
maybe *that's not your Mommy anymore.*

And when this happens, you must go!
Here is how you're sure to know:

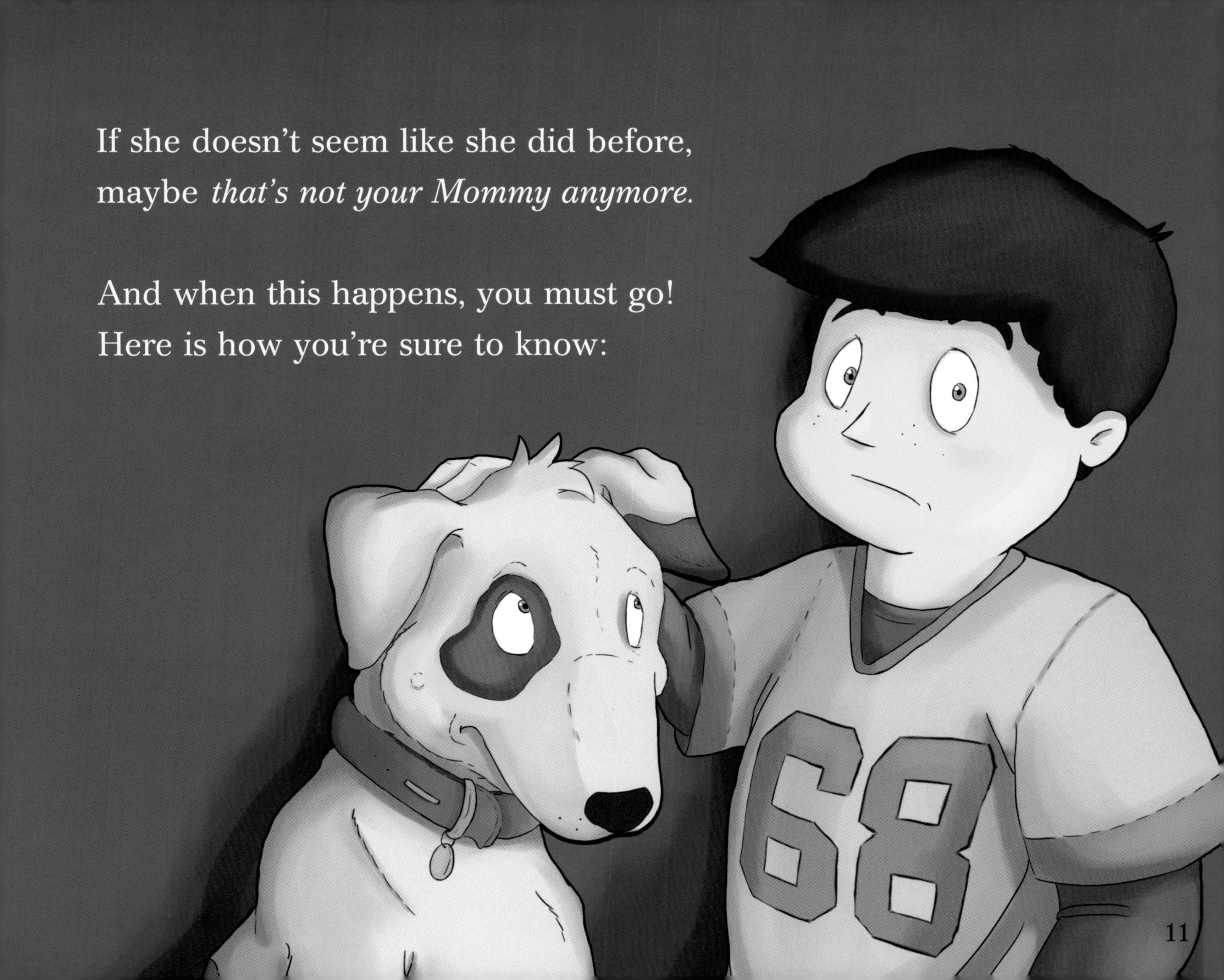
68

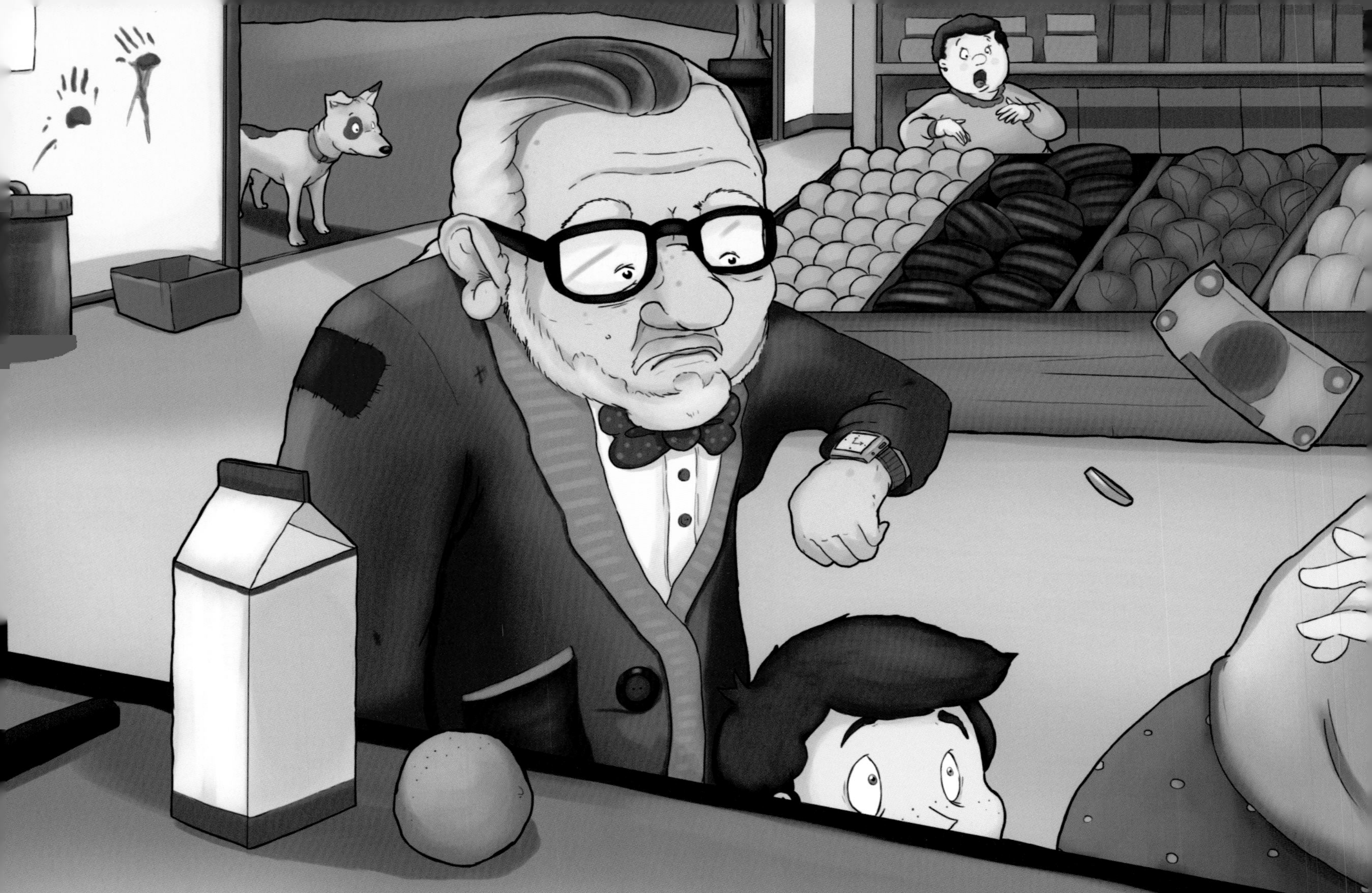

When she bites the checker at the store,

that's not your Mommy anymore.

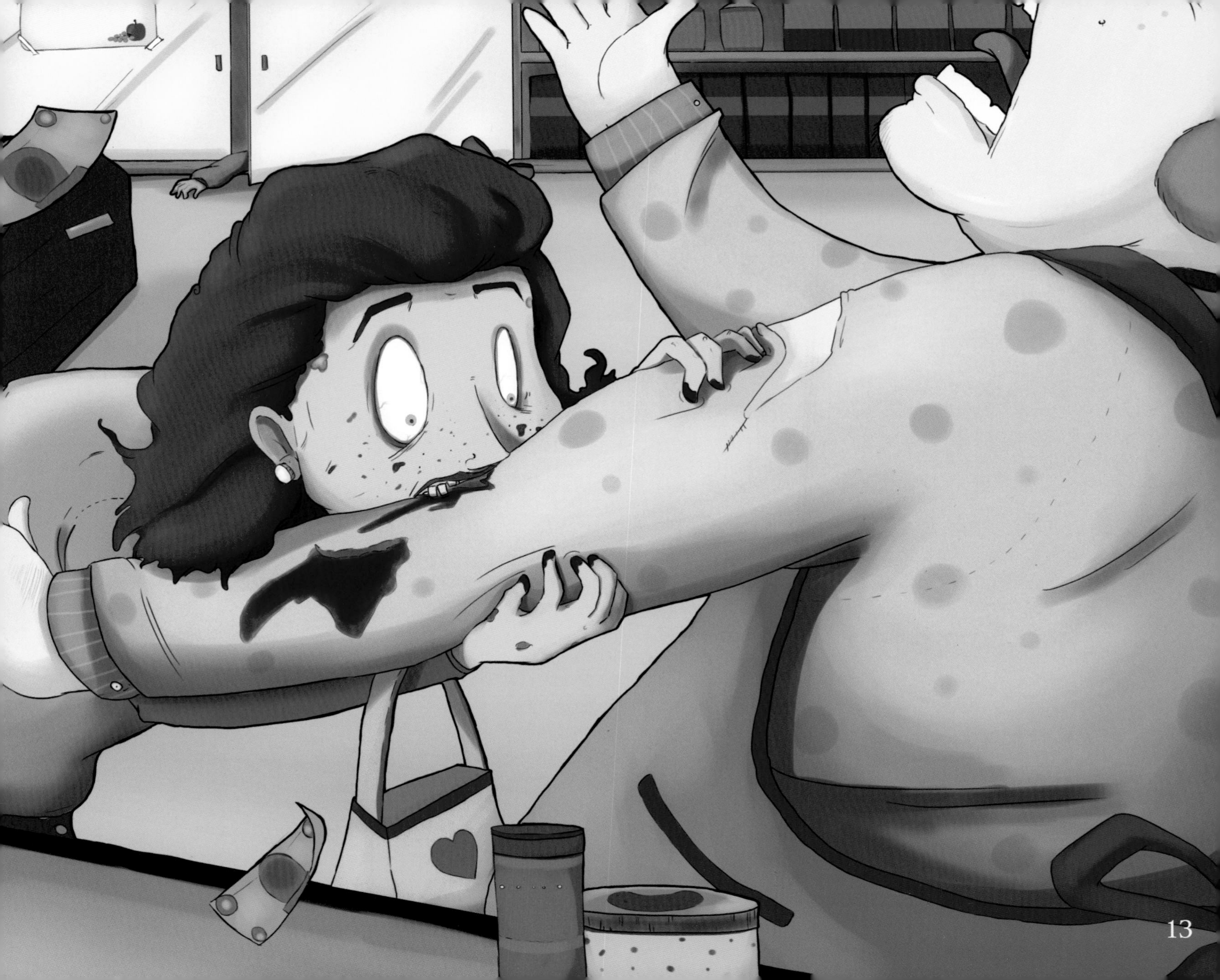

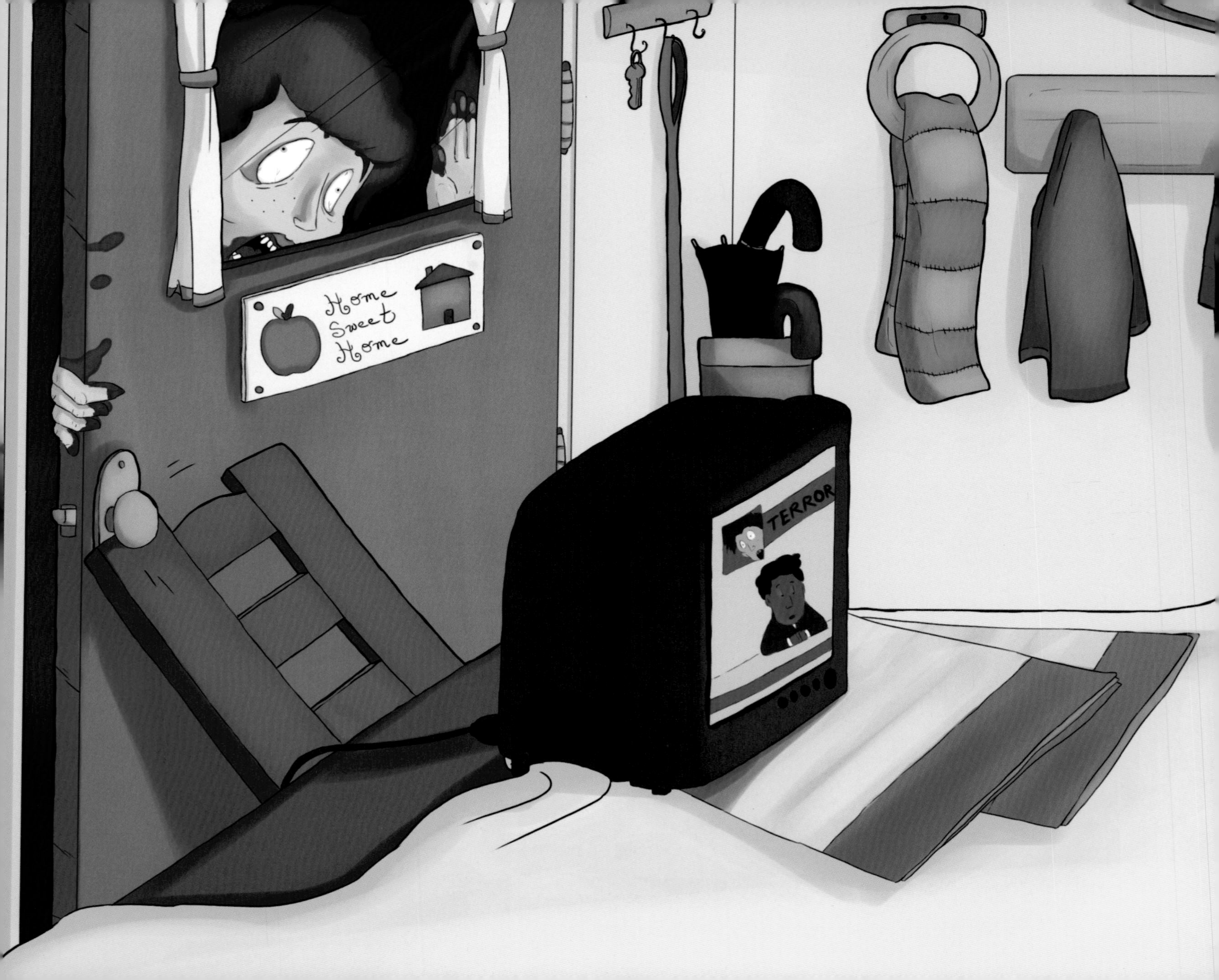
Home
Sweet
Home
TERROR

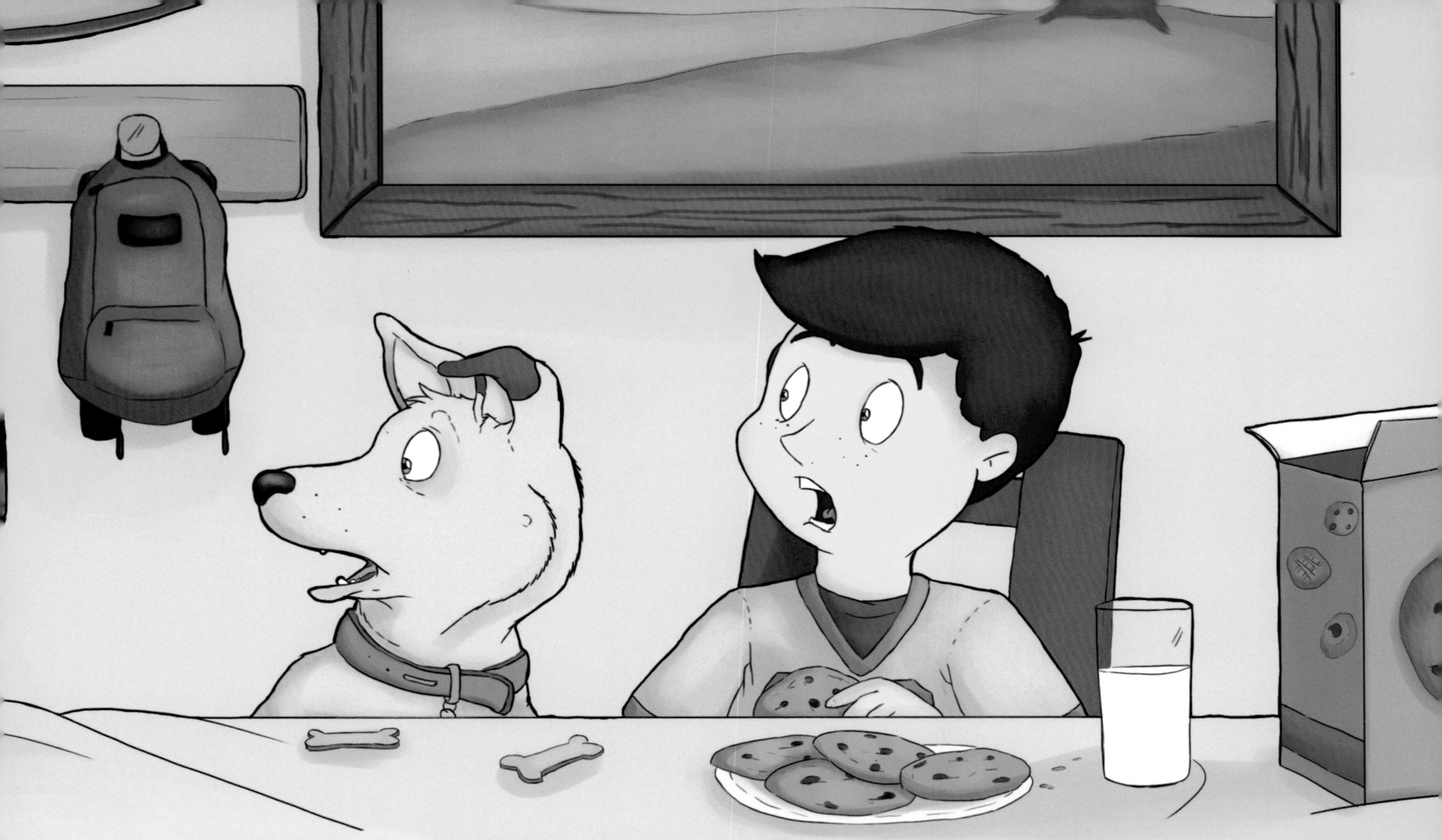

When she's clawing at the kitchen door,
that's not your Mommy anymore.
When her face looks like an apple core,
that's not your Mommy anymore.

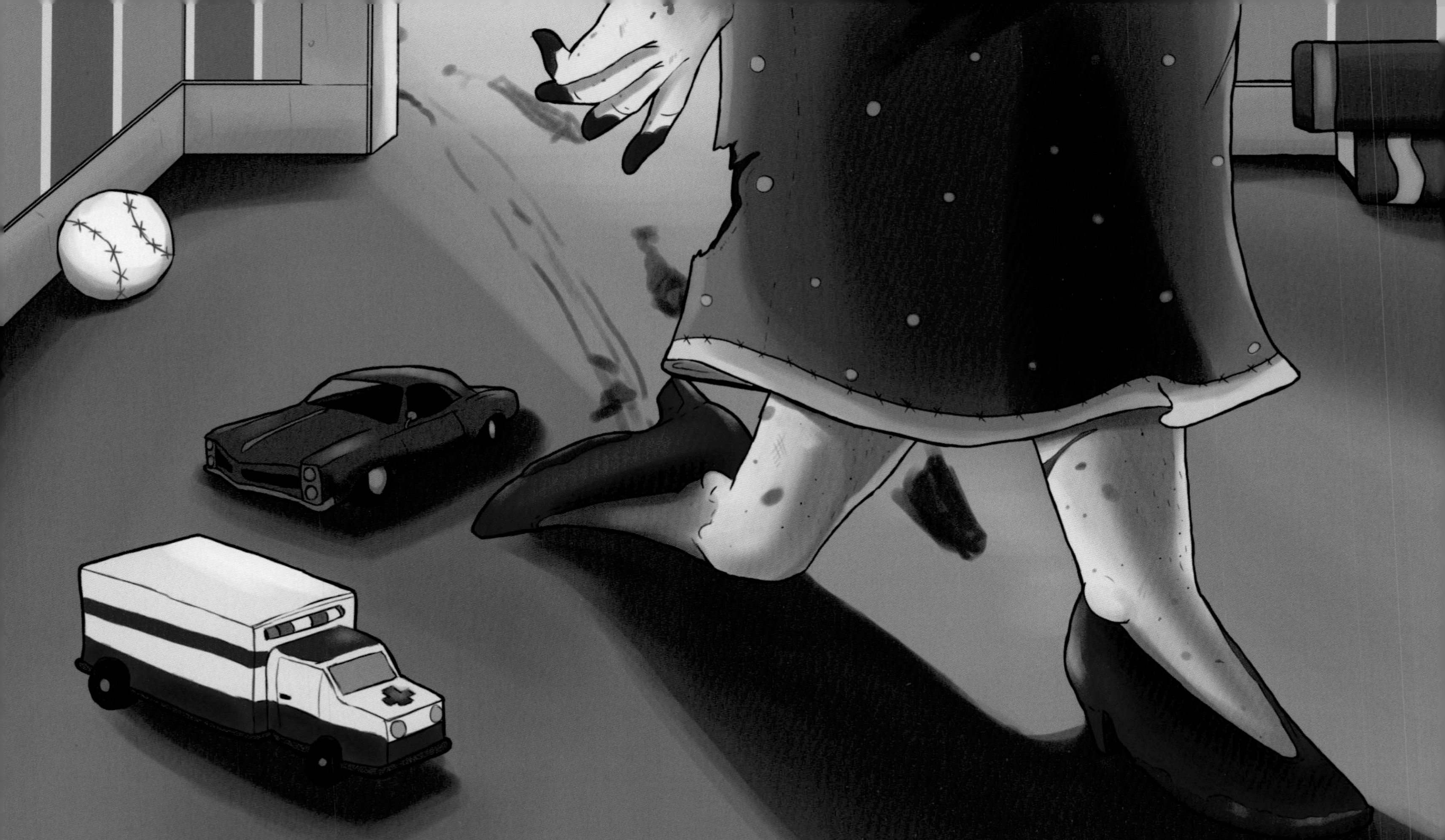

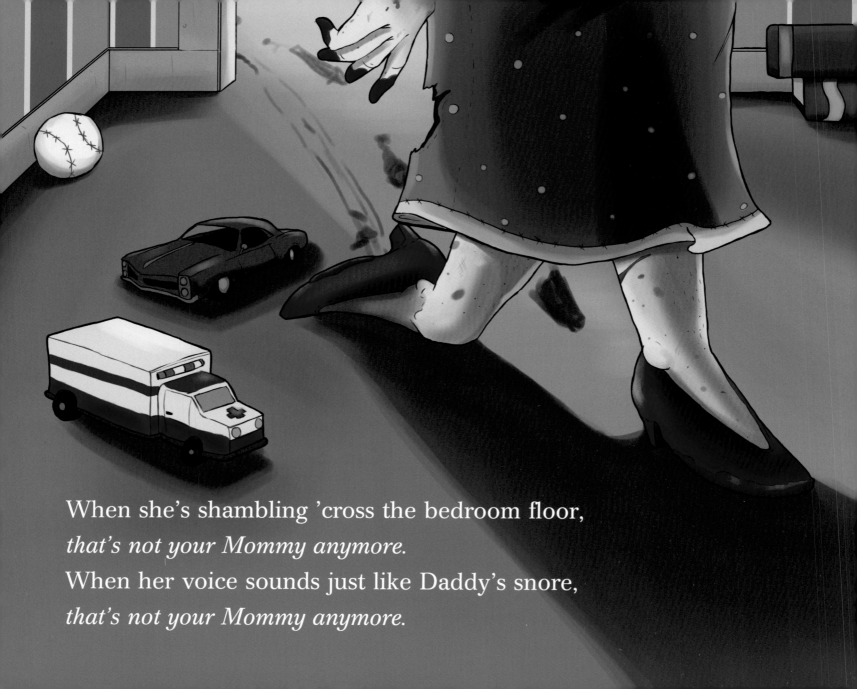

When she's shambling 'cross the bedroom floor,
that's not your Mommy anymore.
When her voice sounds just like Daddy's snore,
that's not your Mommy anymore.

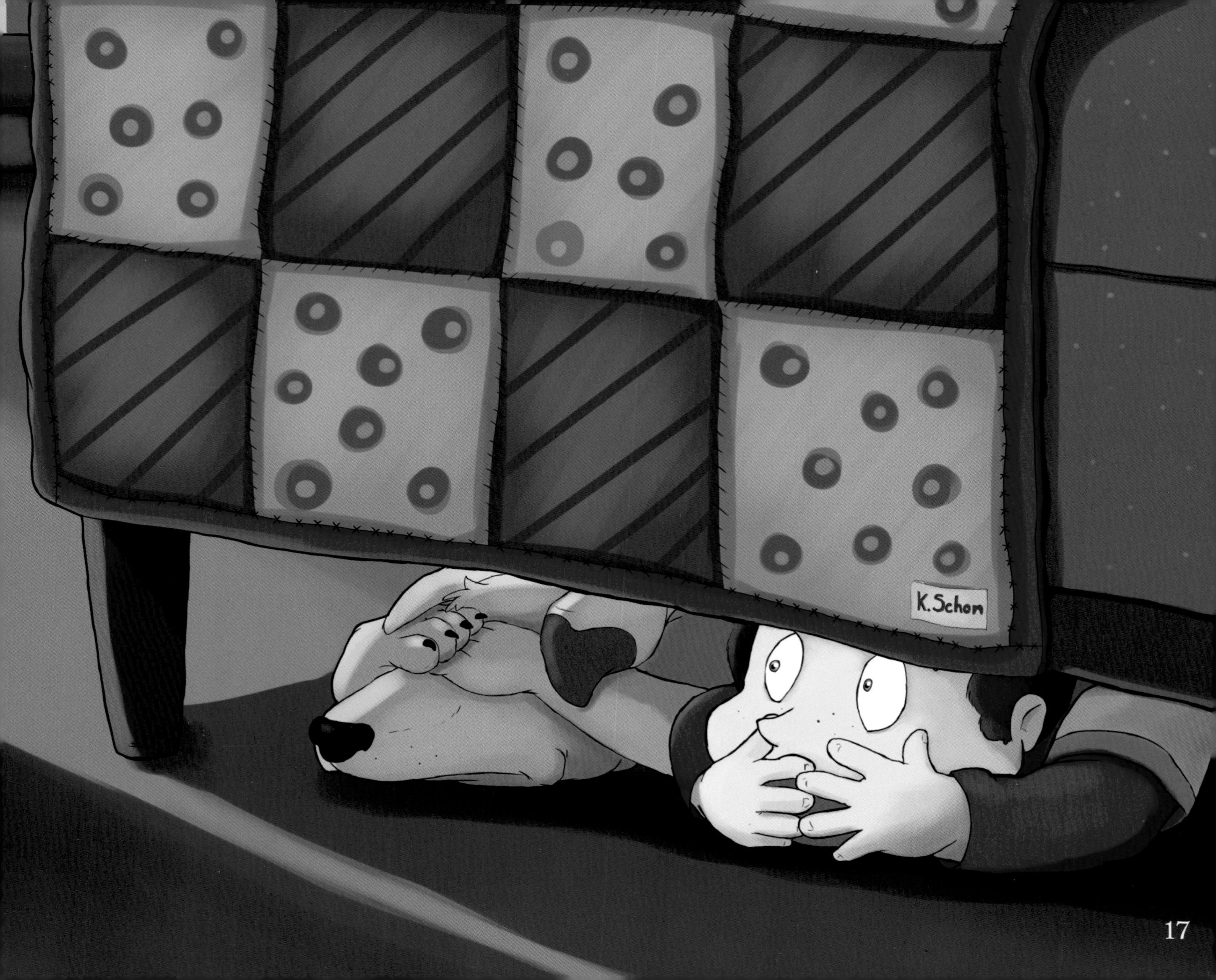
K.Schon

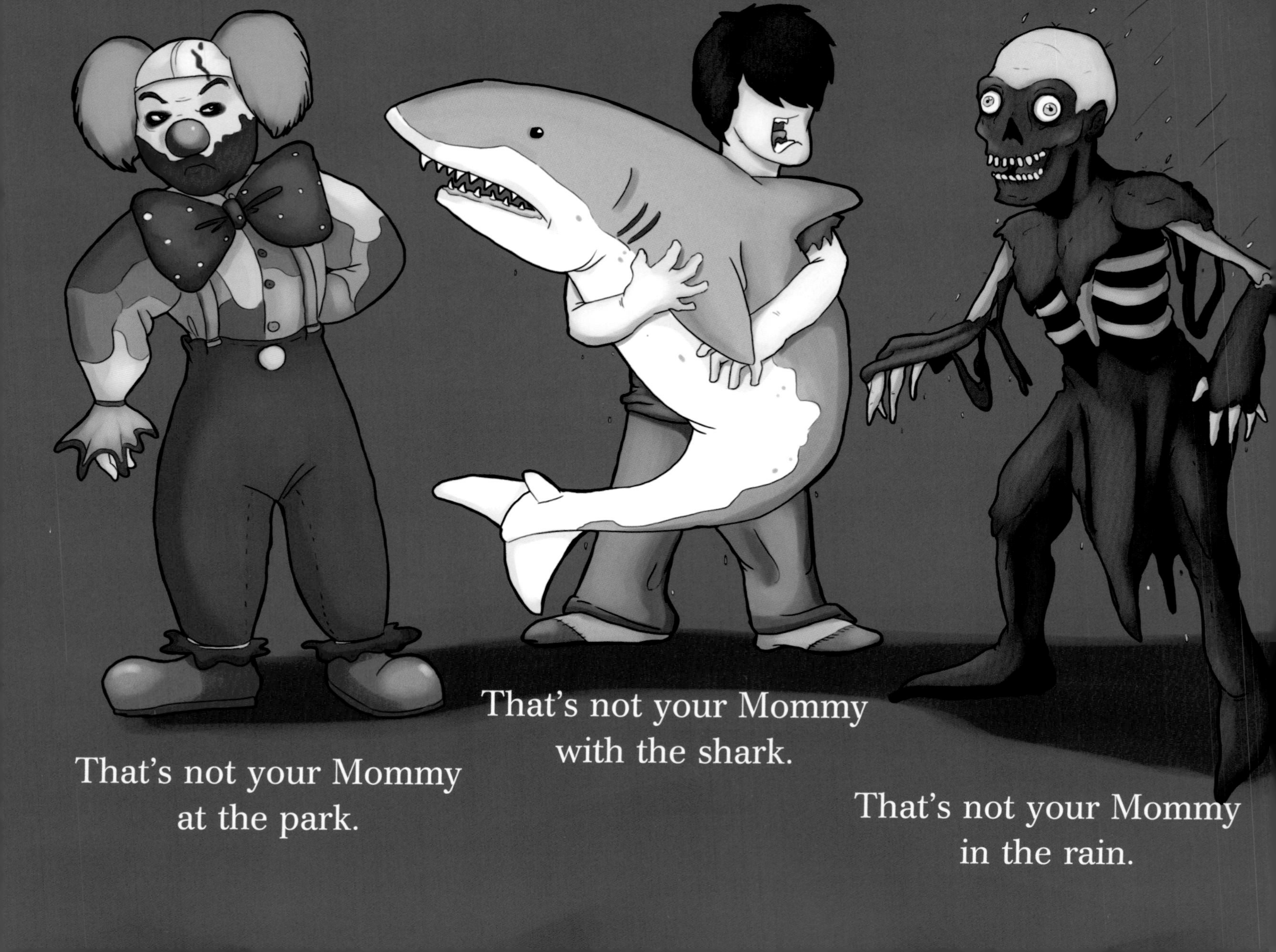

That's not your Mommy
with the shark.

That's not your Mommy
at the park.

That's not your Mommy
in the rain.

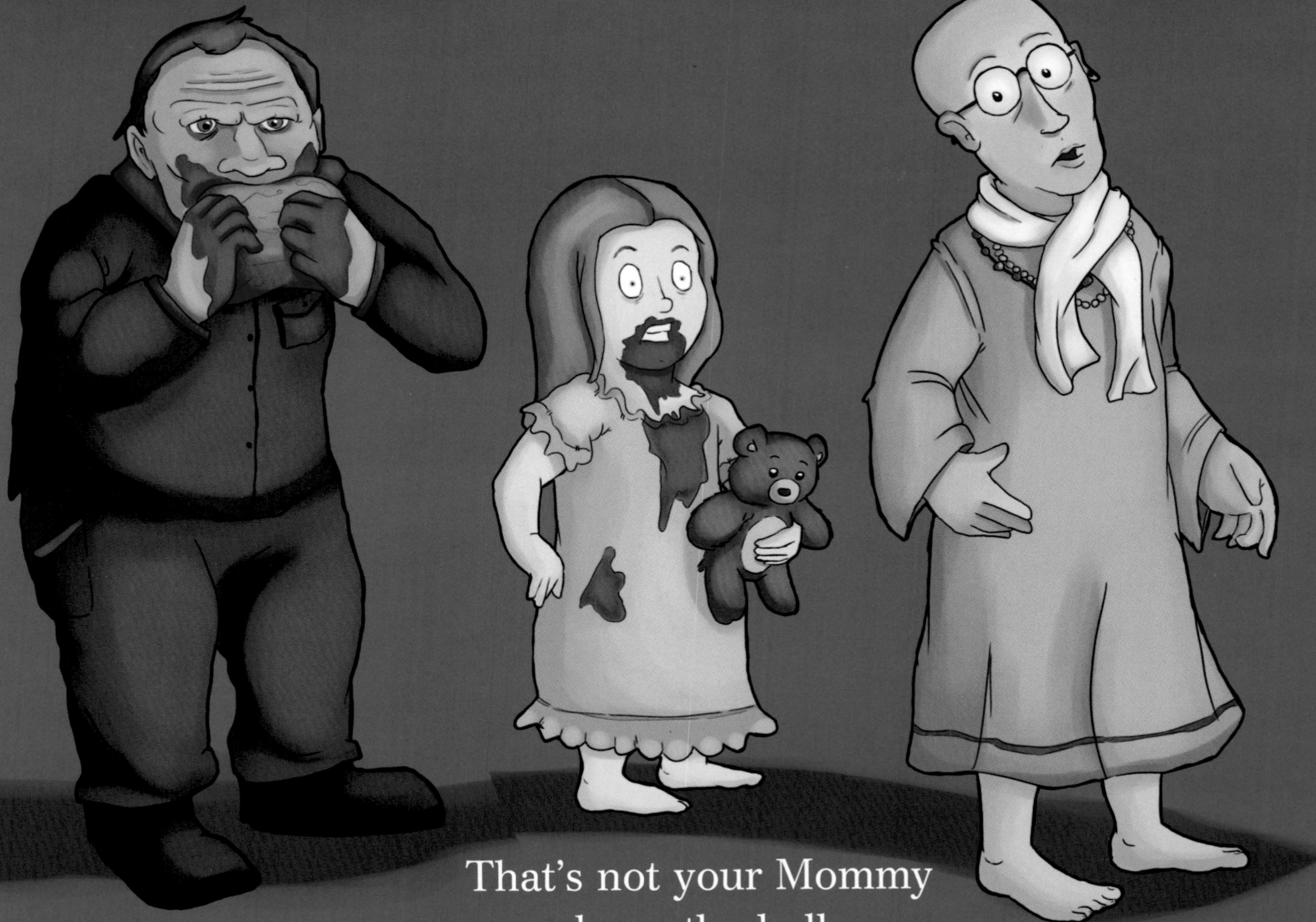

That's not your Mommy
eating brains.

That's not your Mommy
down the hall.

That's not your Mommy
at the mall.

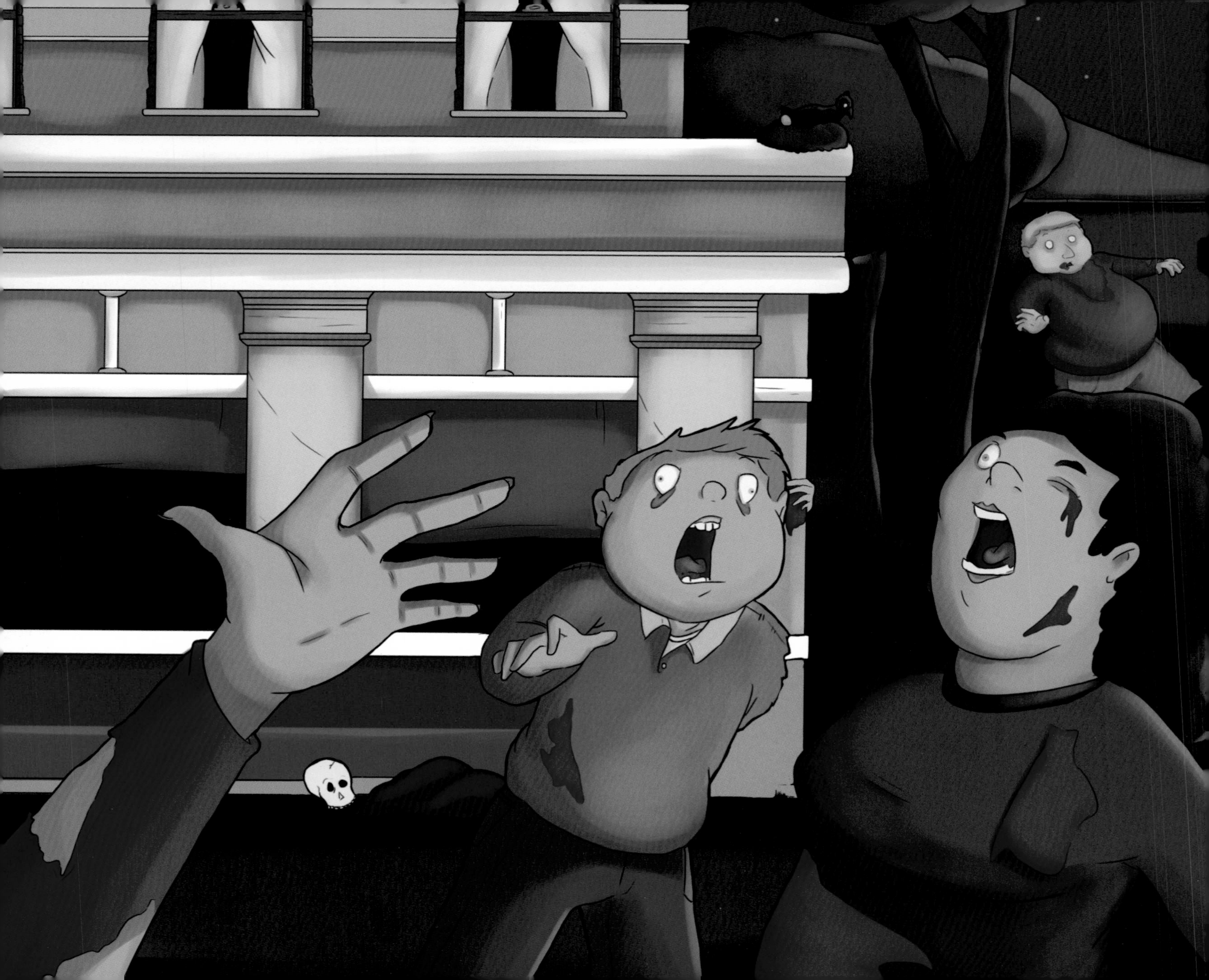

That's not your Mommy over there,
that's not your Mommy EVERYWHERE!

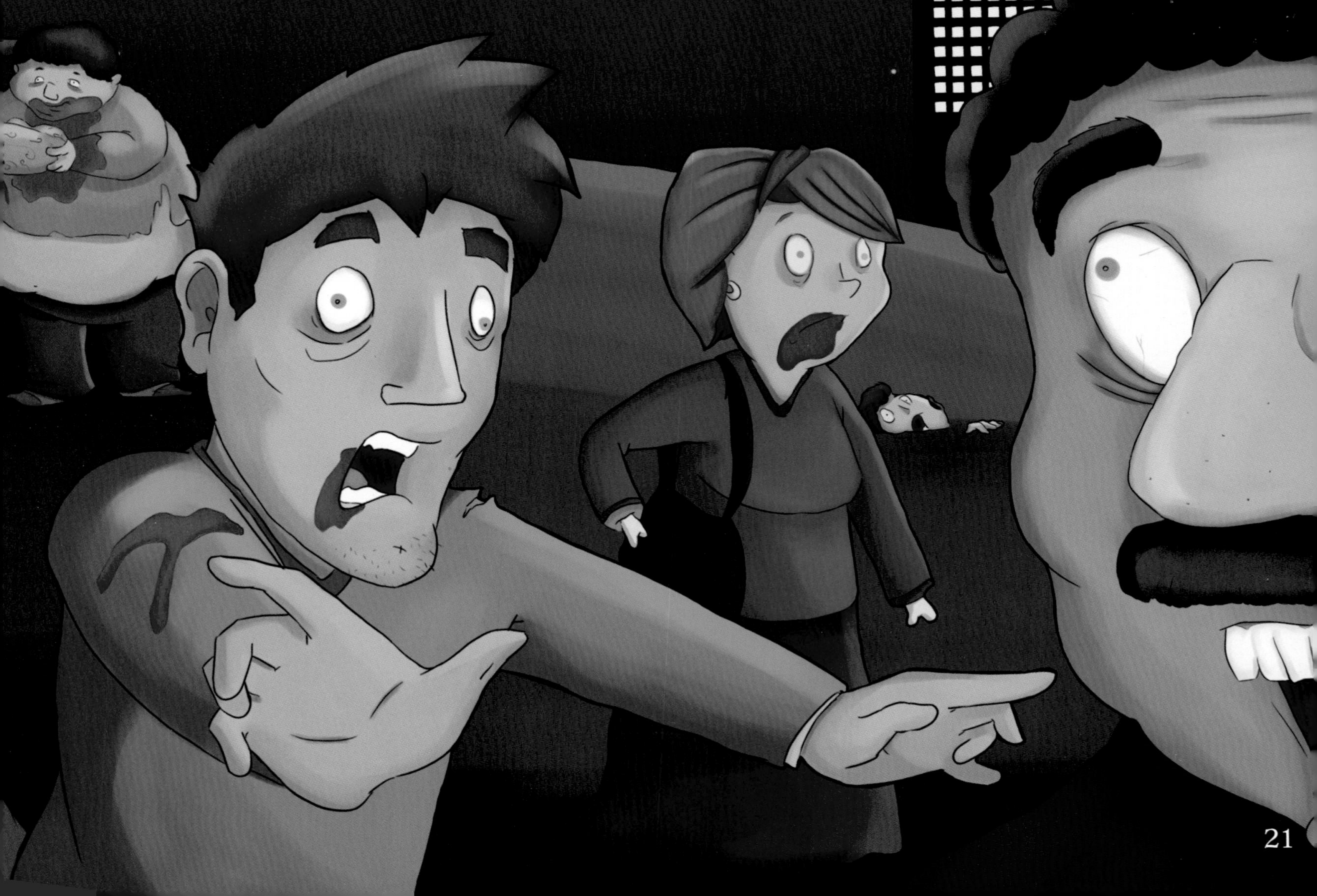

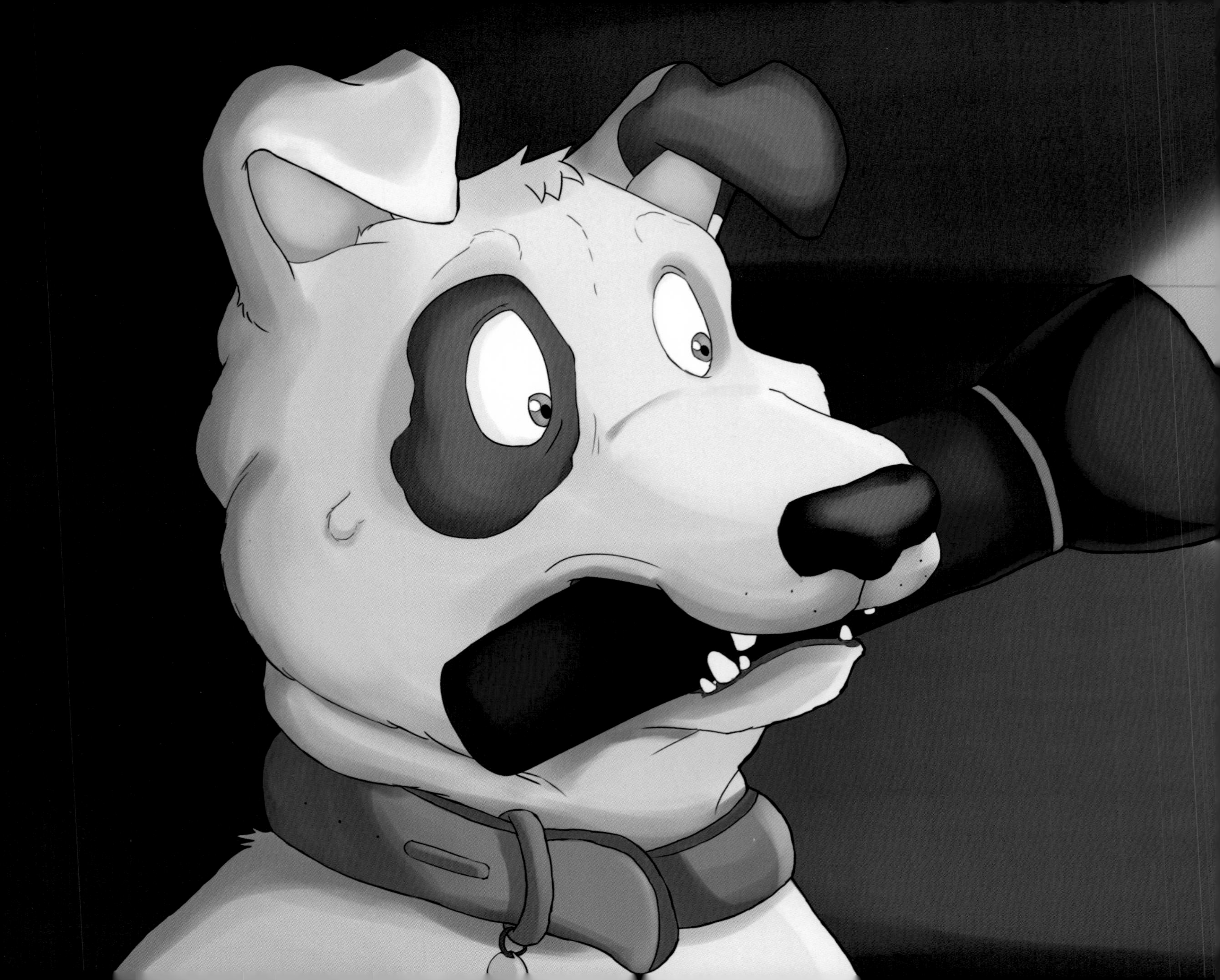

So when this happens and you're sure,
quick, fetch the flashlight from the drawer

and run and hide like never before!

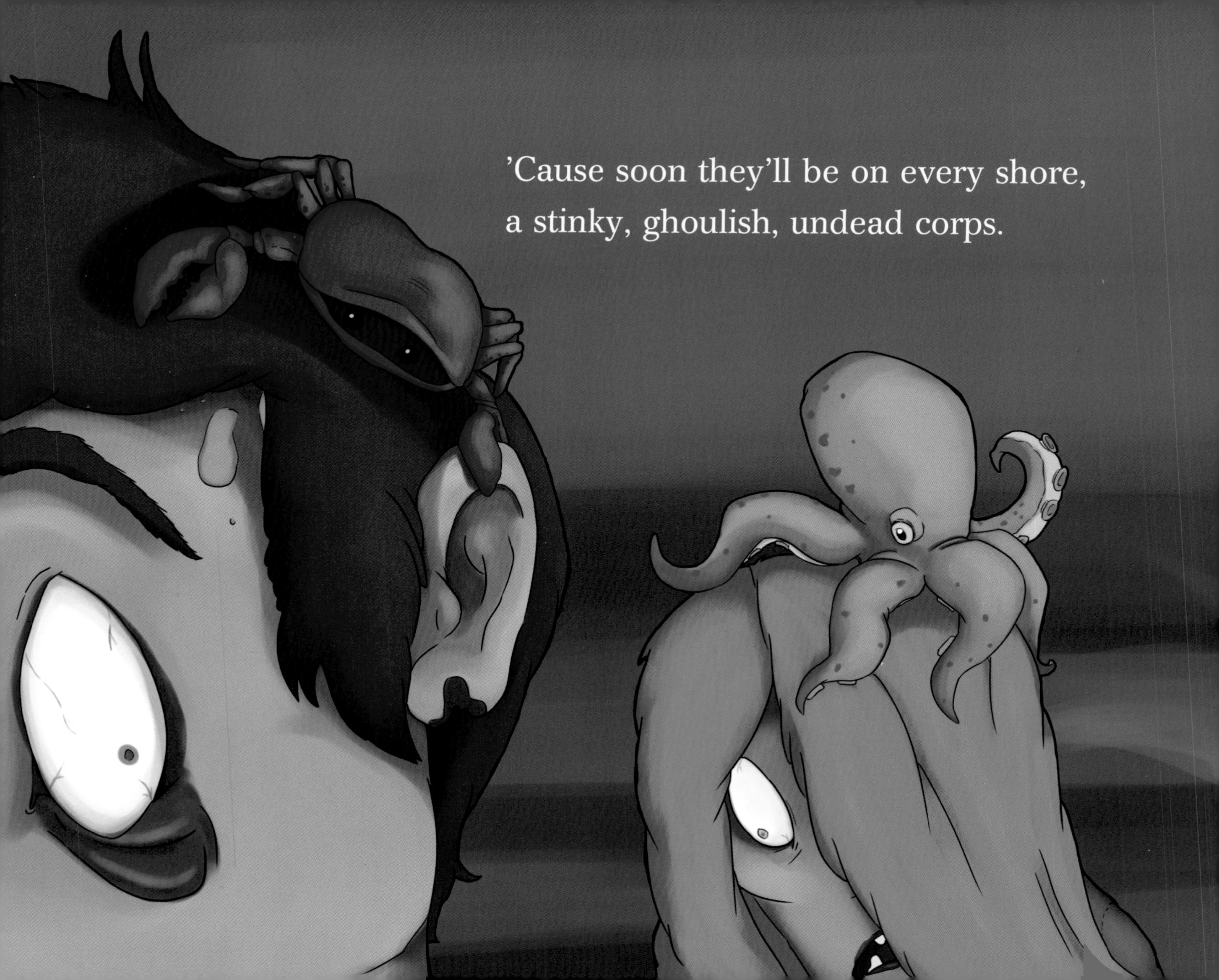

'Cause soon they'll be on every shore,
a stinky, ghoulish, undead corps.

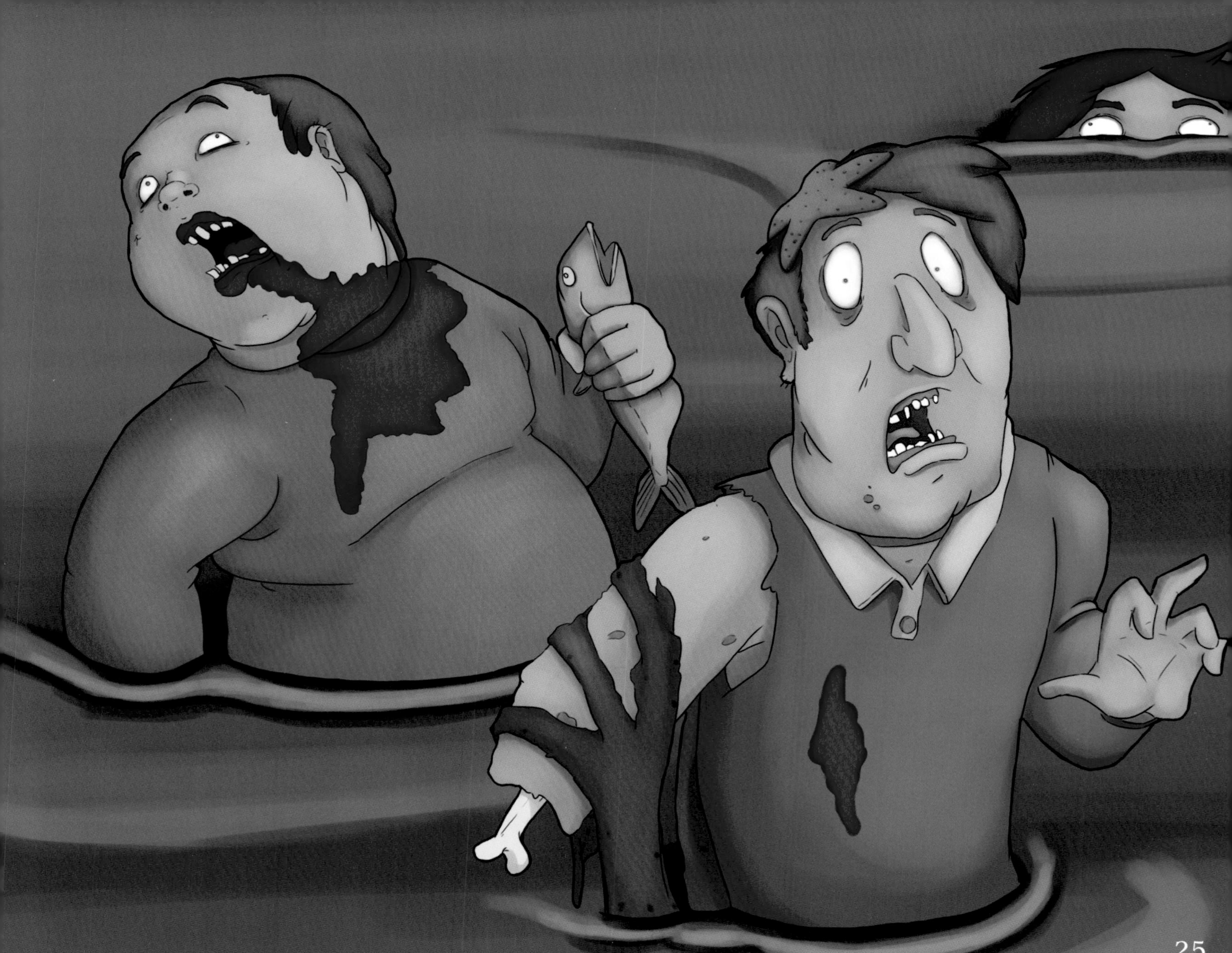

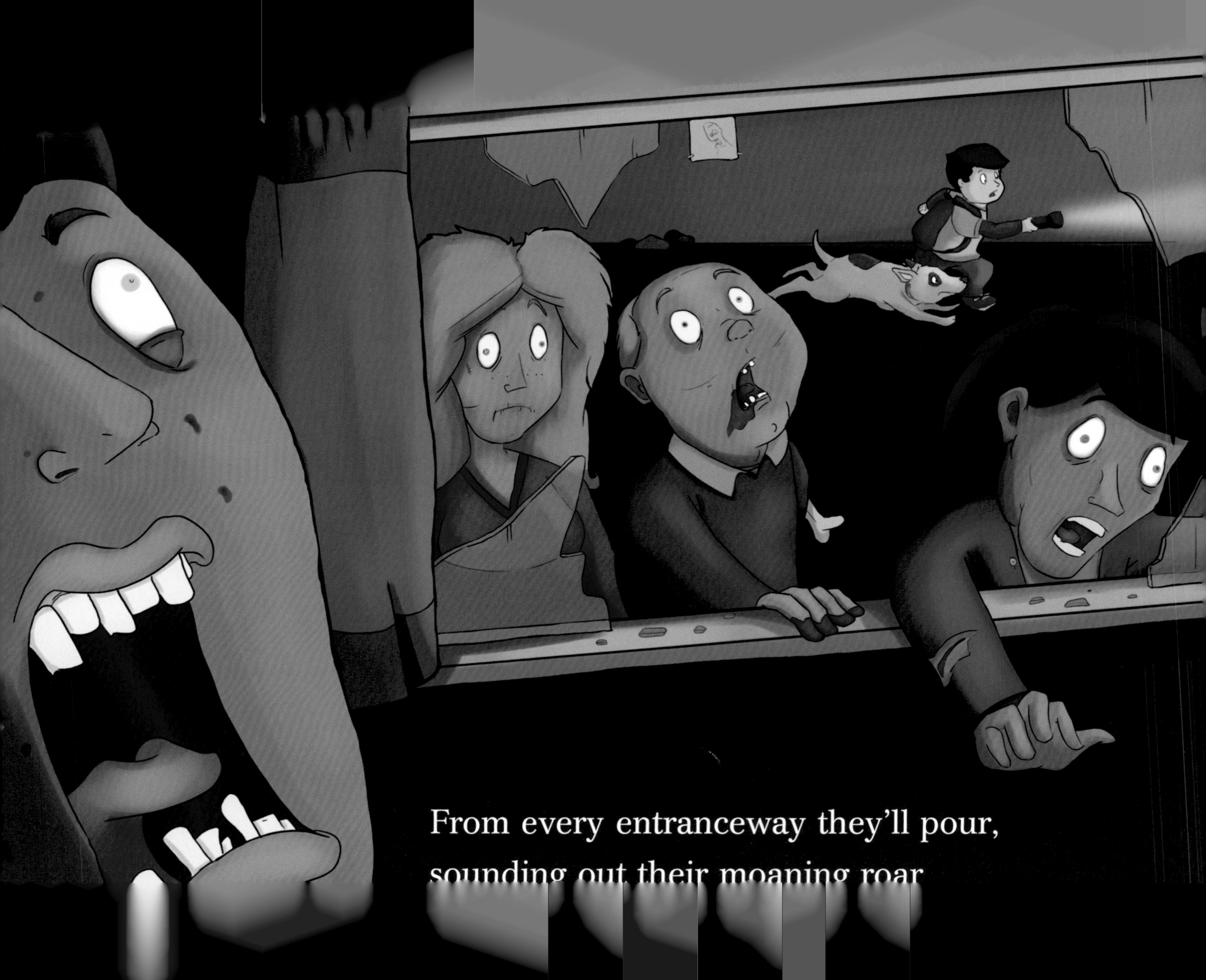

From every entranceway they'll pour,
sounding out their moaning roar

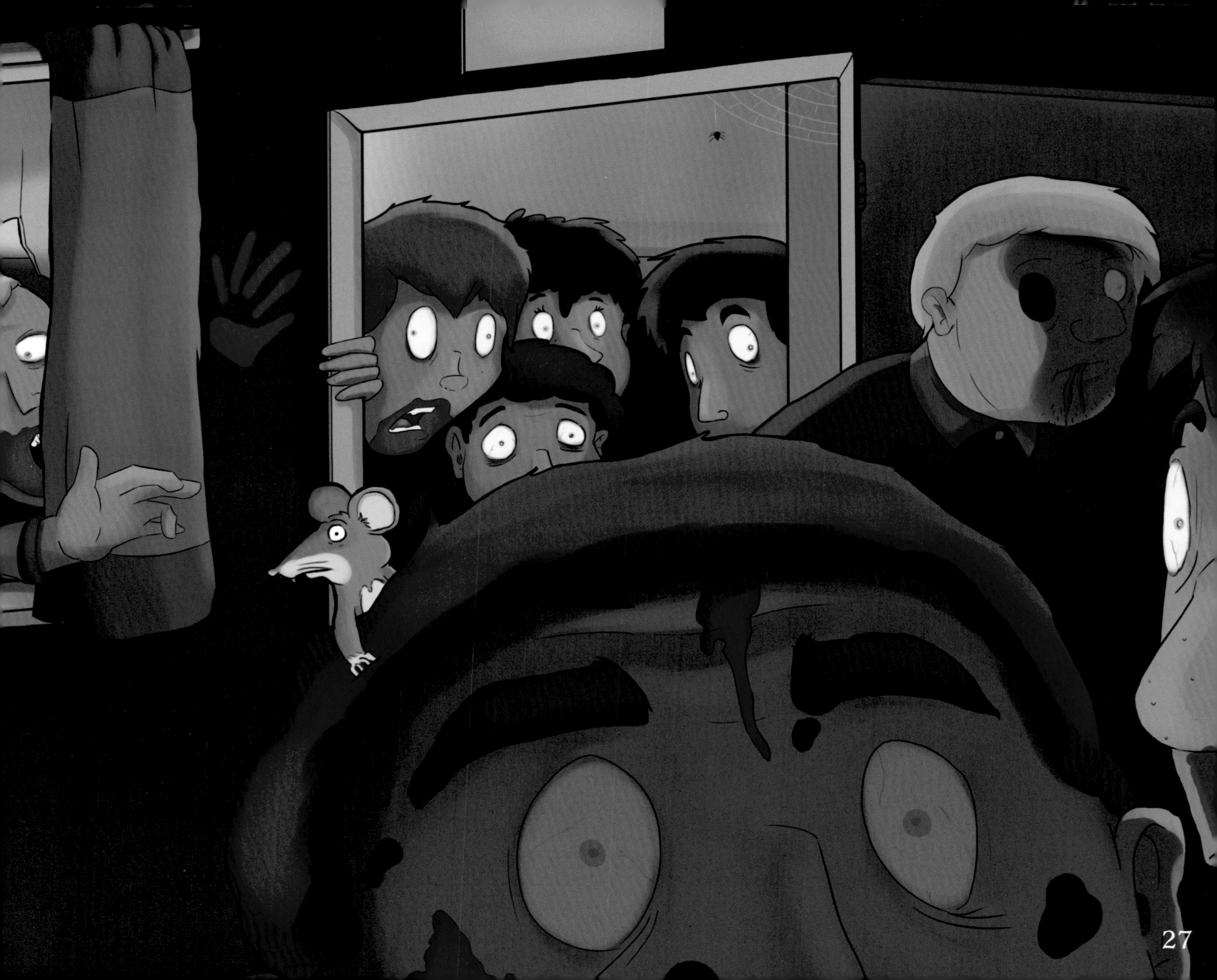

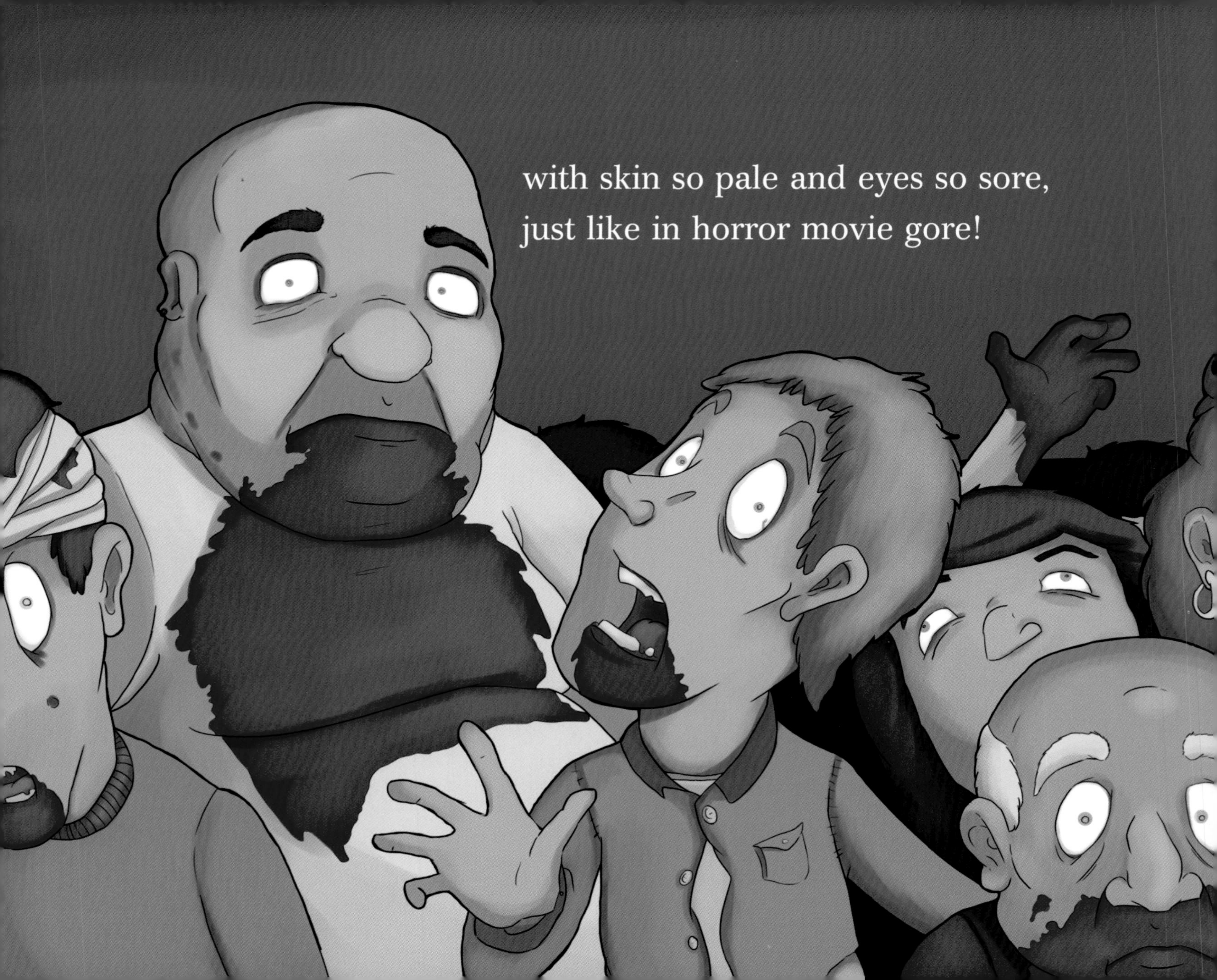

with skin so pale and eyes so sore,
just like in horror movie gore!

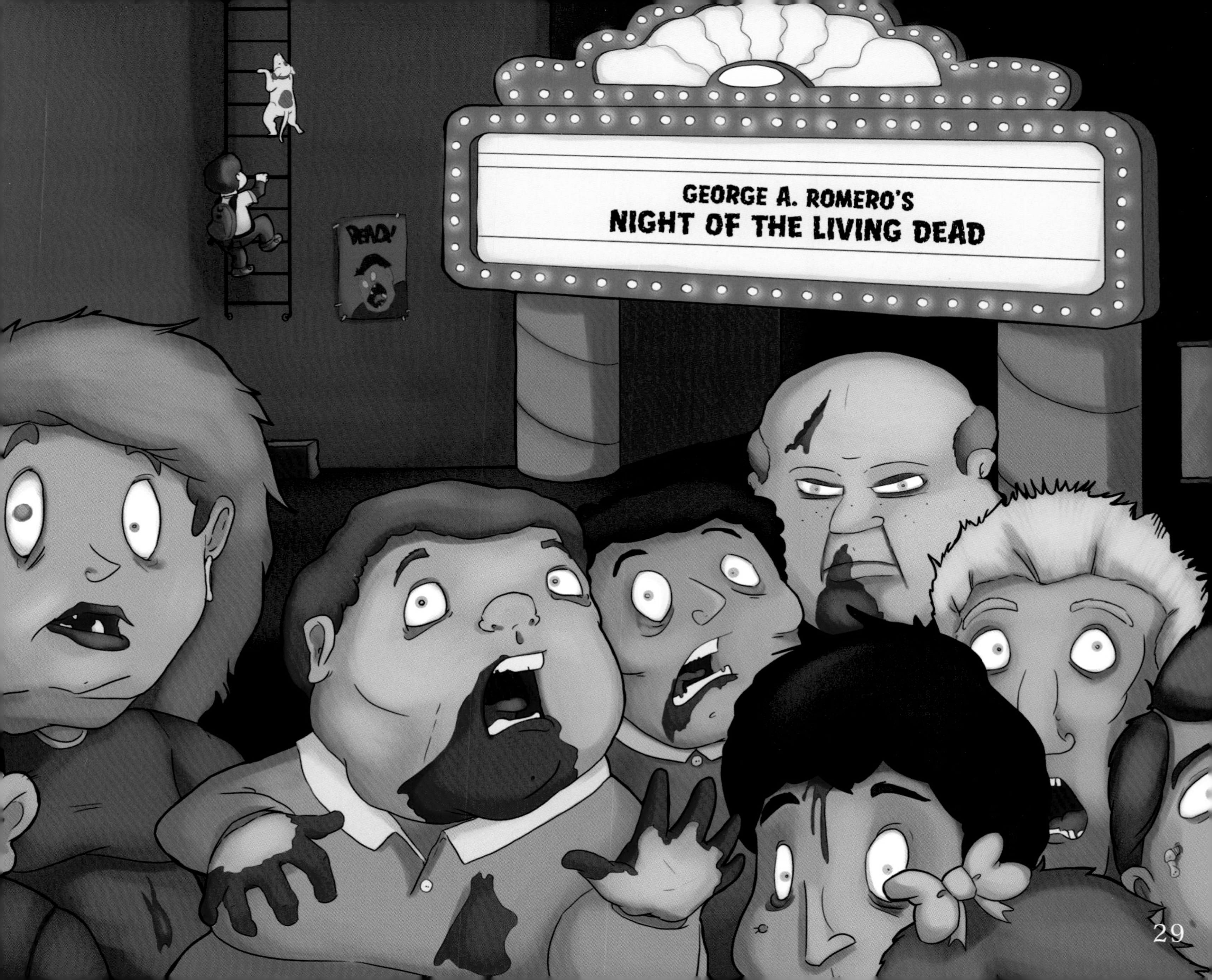

DEAD!
GEORGE A. ROMERO'S
NIGHT OF THE LIVING DEAD

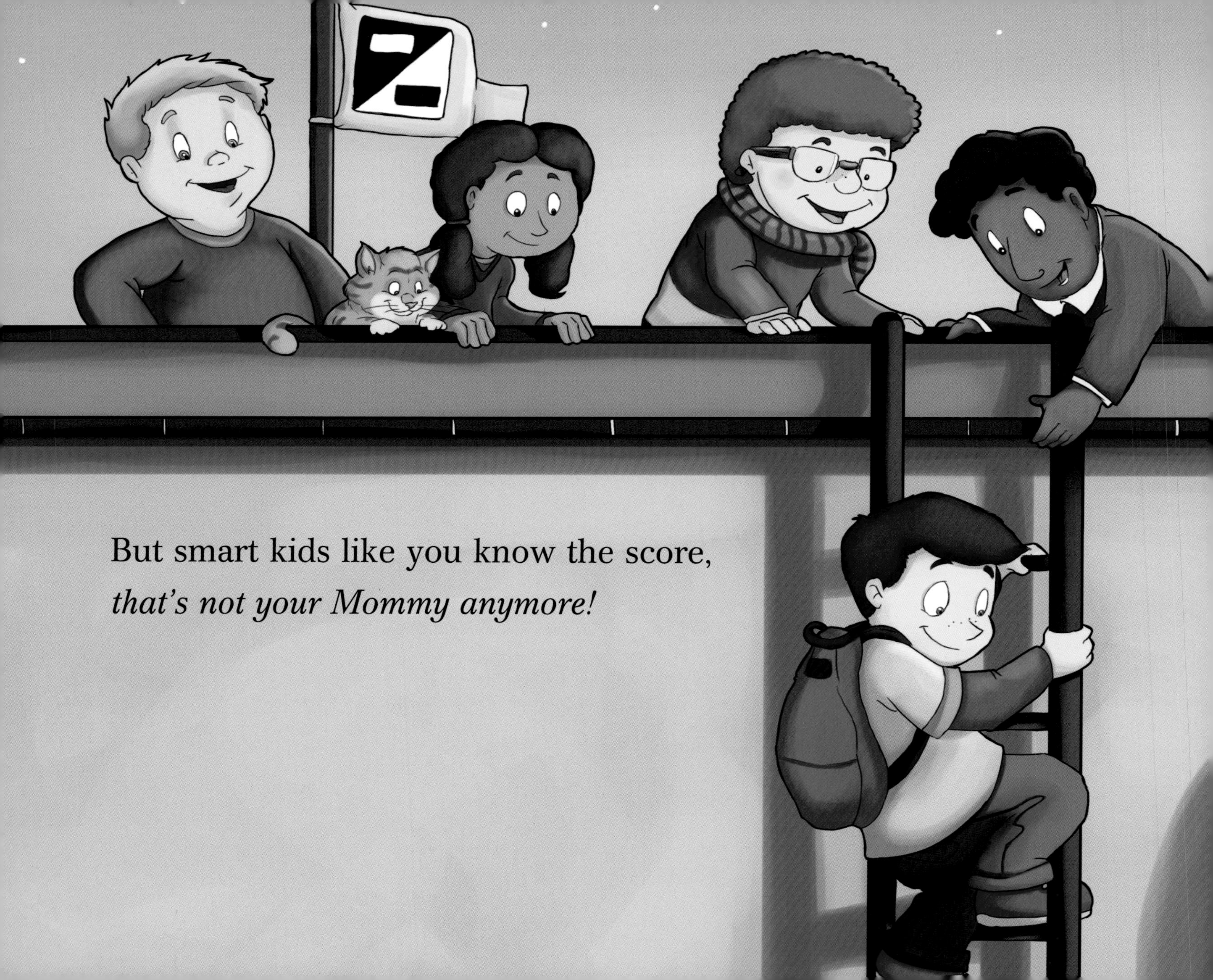

But smart kids like you know the score,
that’s not your Mommy anymore!

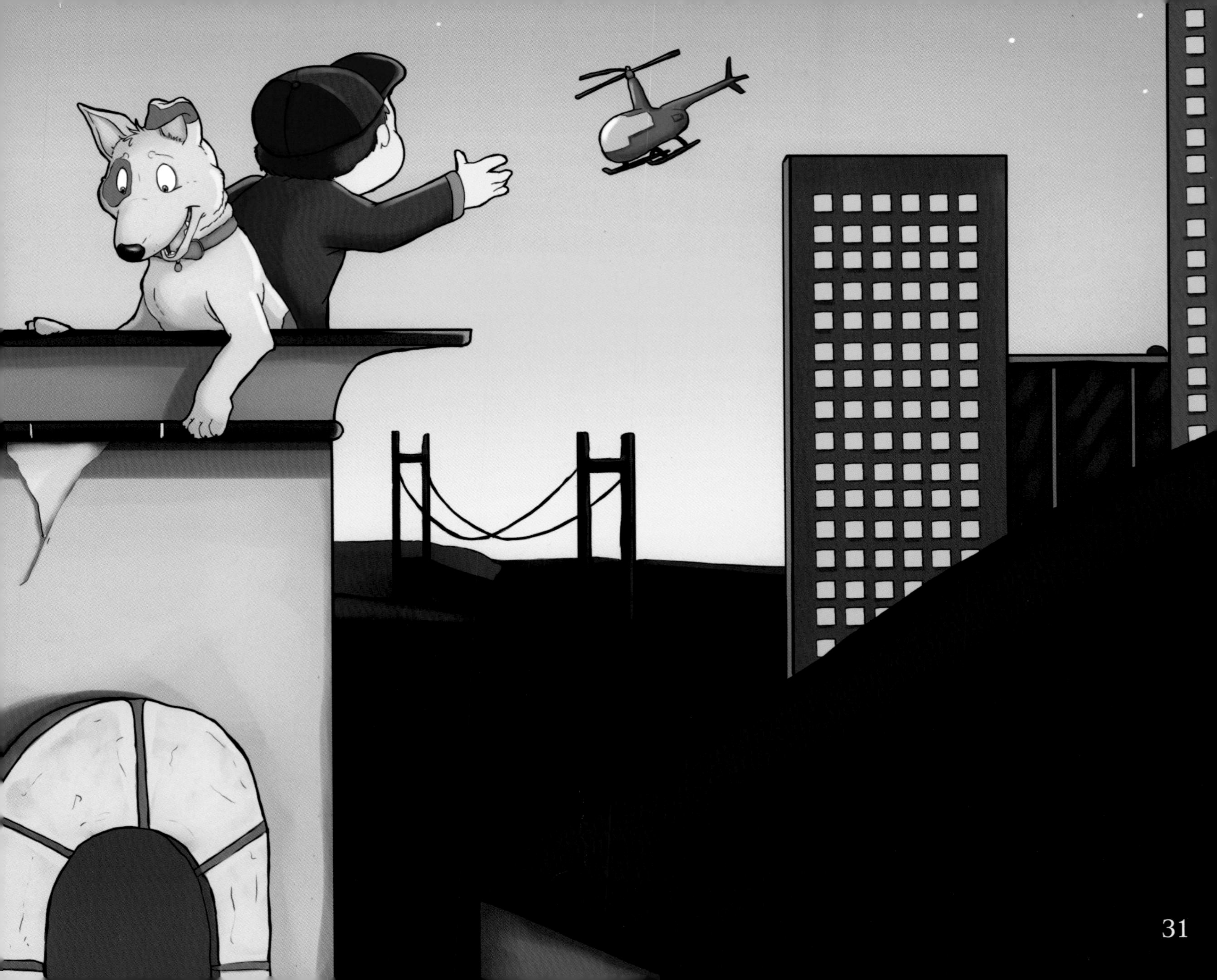

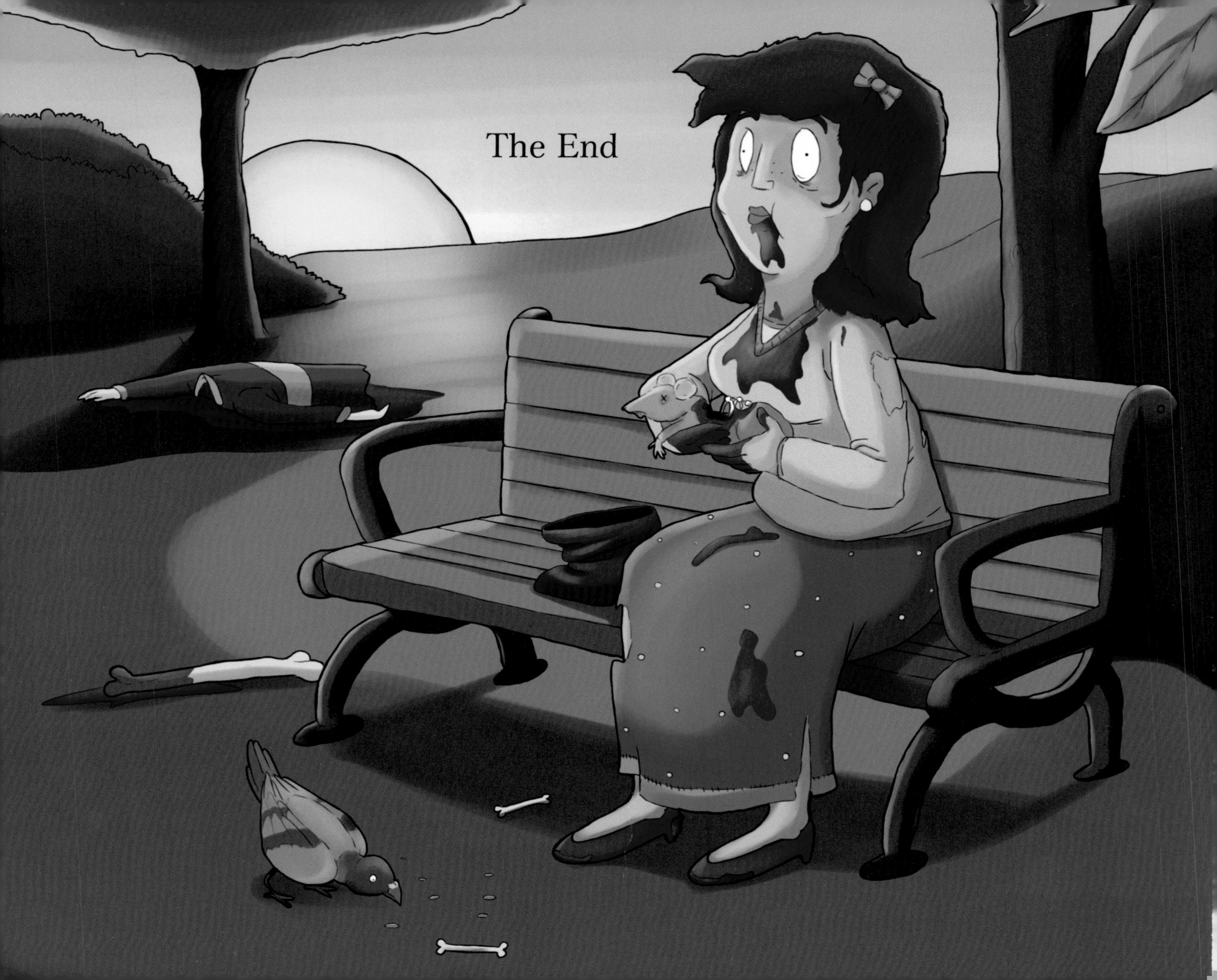
The End